Where Max?

by Diana Noonan
illustrated by Ned Culic

Harcourt
SCHOOL PUBLISHERS

N 10: 0-15-350338-6
N 13: 978-0-15-350338-2

ering Options
N 10: 0-15-350331-9 (Grade 1 Below-Level Collection)
N 13: 978-0-15-350331-3 (Grade 1 Below-Level Collection)
N 10: 0-15-357389-9 (package of 5)
N 13: 978-0-15-357389-7 (package of 5)

5 6 7 8 9 10   179   15 14 13 12 11 10 09 08

Where are you, Max?

I am in here, Dad.

Where are you, Max?

I am in here, Dad.

Come in here, too, Dad.

No, no, no!

Come in here, Max.